and the Temple of Gloom

uGenia Lavender

and the Temple of Gloom

Geri Halliwell

Illustrated by Rian Hughes

MACMILLAN CHILDREN'S BOOKS

This is a work of fiction. These stories, characters, places and events
are all completely made-up, imaginary and absolutely not true.

Ugenia Lavender X

First published 2008 by Macmillan Children's Books
a division of Macmillan Publishers Limited
20 New Wharf Road, London N1 9RR
Basingstoke and Oxford
Associated companies throughout the world
www.panmacmillan.com

ISBN 978-0-230-70145-8

Text and illustrations copyright © Geri Halliwell 2008
Illustrations by Rian Hughes
Brain Squeezers by Amanda Li

The right of Geri Halliwell to be identified as the
author of this work has been asserted by her in accordance
with the Copyright, Designs and Patents Act 1988.

3 5 7 9 8 6 4 2

A CIP catalogue record for this book is available from
the British Library.

Printed and bound in Great Britain by MPG Books Ltd, Bodmin, Cornwall

Contents

To Bluebell. Little girl, big imagination.

1

uGenia Lavender

and the Angry Giant

Ugenia woke up in her usual action-hero,
Hunk Roberts way – leaping over the bed
and dashing straight into the bathroom.
There, she gave herself an extra-special
toothpaste-advert smile as she brushed
her teeth in the mirror. It was the end of
September and a sunny weekend. Ugenia
was really excited, as one of her best friends,
Crazy Trevor, was coming over to play
football on the green.

Ugenia quickly pulled on her clothes and tugged a hairbrush through her hair. She bounded down the stairs just as the front doorbell was ringing. Ugenia opened the door to find Trevor with a football tucked under his arm and a small person standing next to him. It was

Peachy Melba, his half-sister (they had the same mum, but different dads).

'Er, Ugenia, is it all right if I leave Peachy with you for a bit?' asked Trevor. 'I have to go and do something.'

Ugenia looked down at the little girl. She had golden caramel skin and wild frizzy hair.

'Hmm, I don't know. That sounds like a lot of work to me,' said Ugenia.

'If you look after Peachy, you can borrow this amazing leather football,' pleaded Trevor. 'As long as you're careful with it, because my neighbour Spike has lent it to me. I've promised to give it back in one piece, otherwise *he's* promised *me* a black eye.'

Ugenia stared at Peachy Melba, who looked like a scared mouse, and then at the amazing red football.

'Well, perhaps she won't be too much trouble after all,' Ugenia sighed. 'Yeah, sure, I'll look after it *and* your little sister. Hi, Peachy, nice to meet you.'

Peachy Melba said nothing and gave a very timid smile.

'She can be a little tricky,' whispered Trevor as he handed over Peachy Melba and the red leather football, then quickly backed away.

'You don't seem tricky to me,' Ugenia said to Peachy Melba as she closed the door behind Trevor. 'You're just a bit shy, right? OK now, Peachy, would you like to visit Granny Betty's house for a game of footy? She's my really cool great-grandmother, who's 101 years old but doesn't act it, that's for sure!'

Peachy Melba still said nothing and gave another very timid smile.

'OK, I'll take that as a yes then,' said Ugenia, taking Peachy's hand. Grabbing her house keys, Ugenia closed the door behind her before walking over to her gran's house, just around the corner.

Granny Betty lived in a decrepit little cottage with a rusty old car in the front garden that hadn't been driven for years. Next door to her was a very large house that was almost completely hidden by

very high red-brick walls. There was an
enormous magnolia tree which seemed
to be creeping over the walls as if it was
peering into Granny Betty's garden, and a
new sign that said:

KEEP OUT – INTRUDERS ENTER
AT YOUR OWN RISK

Just as Ugenia was about to go into Granny
Betty's house, something next door caught
her attention
– a large wooden
door in the wall
creaked opened.
Ugenia stared as
a gigantic nose
curled round it,

followed by a huge hand, then suddenly the
door was slammed shut and whoever it was
disappeared behind it again.

Peachy Melba said nothing, but gave a
very frightened smile and trembled as she
stared at the high walls guarding Granny
Betty's neighbour's property.

'Hmm, I wonder who that was?' Ugenia
looked puzzled. 'I bet my Granny Betty will
know,' she said as she rang the
doorbell.

A couple of minutes
later they could hear
heels tottering down the
hallway and then the door
was flung open. Granny
Betty threw her arms around
Ugenia and gave her a hug

that was just a little bit too hard.

'Come in, come in! You're just in time for tea and Christmas cake!' she announced (even though it clearly wasn't Christmas, it was actually early autumn!).

'Hello, Granny, meet Peachy Melba,' said Ugenia.

'Hello, my dear Peachy, how are you?' said Granny Betty.

Peachy said nothing and gave a very timid smile.

'She's Crazy Trevor's half-sister,' explained Ugenia. 'And a little shy.'

Ugenia and Peachy Melba walked into Granny Betty's living room, which smelt a bit of mothballs. There were two large red armchairs beside a gas fire. One was empty, but in the other was Mrs Wisteria, Granny

Betty's neighbour from across the road – a very skinny woman with her hair pulled tightly into a bun. She was drinking a cup of tea from a yellow china cup and had her white poodle, Rupert, at her feet. She looked as if she had just sucked a rather sour lemon.

'Hello, Mrs Wisteria,' said Ugenia. 'Hello, Rupert,' she added, patting the dog's head. 'This is my friend Peachy Melba.'

Peachy Melba said nothing and gave a timid smile.

'Now, tell me what's been going on with you. I want to know everything!' said Granny Betty as she sliced Ugenia and Peachy Melba a piece of Christmas cake.

'Well, actually, Gran, I want to know about your new neighbour with the big hands and large nose?' said Ugenia. 'I've never seen him before. What's behind the high brick walls? And why the big sign?'

Mrs Wisteria spat out her tea and dropped her yellow cup on the floor as she began to choke on her Christmas cake.

'You don't want to go meddling with the likes of him – that man's a monster! He's evil! Stay away from him!' she spat in between swallowing the last few mouthfuls of cake. 'He's an angry giant who would eat up someone like you for breakfast.'

'An angry giant?' gasped Ugenia.

Peachy Melba began to tremble in terror.

'Now now, that's enough, Mrs Wisteria,' said Granny Betty. 'He's a bit of a mystery, that's for sure, but we don't need to frighten the children.'

Granny Betty decided it was best to change the subject and talk about something different. 'Lovely weather we're having, aren't we?' she said as she readjusted her large, floppy orange sun hat (even though she was indoors).

'Yes, marvellous,' said Mrs Wisteria as she began to discuss the price of milk or something that sounded like 'blah blah blah' to Ugenia.

Ugenia felt very bored, so she decided to lead Peachy Melba out into the garden.

'Peachy Melba and I are going to play some footy, Granny Betty,' she called over her shoulder. 'Fancy a game?'

'Ooh, I'd love to, but I've really got to work on my indoor cartwheels,' said Granny Betty. 'But you go ahead and have a kickabout.'

So Ugenia and Peachy Melba took the amazing red leather football and began kicking it about in Granny's back garden. It was a large patch of grass that curved round the side of the cottage before joining the front garden where the rusty car was parked. The back garden also had a vegetable patch and a few rose bushes that climbed up the next-door neighbour's tall red-brick walls.

'I wonder what it would be like to meet

this angry giant,' said Ugenia as she kicked the ball to Peachy Melba. 'Probably really scary!'

Peachy Melba said nothing, but gave a trembling smile as she kicked the ball feebly back to Ugenia.

'I wonder how he eats little children for breakfast? Does he smell them out with his big nose? And then snap them with his huge

hands? And cook them in the oven?' said Ugenia as she kicked the ball back again to Peachy Melba.

Peachy Melba said nothing and gave a look of terror, but this time she whacked the amazing red leather football back so hard it flew straight over Ugenia's head, over the high red-brick wall, and straight into the angry giant's property. There was an almighty crash. Ugenia and Peachy Melba heard the sound of breaking glass.

'Oh my goodness!' cried Ugenia. 'Peachy! What have you done?'

Peachy Melba, still shaking, said nothing.

'We have to get the ball back!' Ugenia cried.

Peachy Melba said nothing as her eyes began to fill up with tears.

'Look, don't cry, we can sort this out. I just need to have a think,' said Ugenia, who really had no idea how she was going to fix it. She was either going to have to face the angry giant, or Trevor would have to face Spike empty-handed and get a black eye.

'Either way we're all in big trouble,' sighed Ugenia as she stared at the high walls, and wandered down the side of the cottage to the front part of her granny's garden.

Ugenia stared at the rusty old car and the KEEP OUT sign and the large magnolia tree peering over the high red walls.

What would Hunk Roberts, her favourite action hero, do at a time like this? thought Ugenia.

Then, suddenly, like a thunderbolt of
lightning, Ugenia had a brainwave.

'Ingenious! Wall jump!' she cried as she
leaped on the rusty old car and grabbed
a branch from the magnolia tree. To her

surprise, Peachy Melba followed her and
lunged on to the back of Ugenia's luminous
yellow rucksack.

Ugenia and Peachy flew through the air,
over the KEEP OUT sign, over the high
red wall and down on to the angry giant's
property.

They landed with a thud to find
exactly what was hiding behind the high
red-brick walls — a secret garden. There
were weeping willows, the tallest oak
trees, rambling bushes, gardenias, golden
dewdrops, honeysuckle, hundreds of roses in
every colour and a trickling stream running
gently on to a beautiful manicured lawn.

'Wow!' said Ugenia to Peachy Melba.
'Isn't this amazing!'

Ugenia brushed off the leaves and twigs

17

from herself and Peachy Melba and they ventured further into the garden.

Suddenly, there in front of them, was a ginormous grey house that looked a little bit tired. Through a broken glass window Ugenia could just see a glimpse of a red football,

which sat triumphantly high in some sort of metal pot on a huge wooden table.

'The football!' cried Ugenia.

Ugenia carried on creeping forward, taking a trembling Peachy Melba by the hand through the bushes towards the angry giant's house. 'Come on, Peachy, I know you're scared, but we have to get your brother's ball back otherwise he's in big trouble. You don't want that now, do you?'

Peachy Melba said nothing, gave a very scared smile and carried on following Ugenia towards the house. As they approached the broken window, Ugenia could see that the red leather football, which was on the huge kitchen table, had actually landed in a large cooking pot that was as big as a bath, filled with creamy mashed potatoes. Beside it there was a large plate, just as big, with a huge knife and fork.

'Hmm, I wonder if he's had his lunch yet?' said Ugenia, thinking aloud. 'I hope so, then at least he won't be hungry.' She tried not to think about the angry giant eating small children. Being crunched up with

mashed potatoes wouldn't be much fun.

As Ugenia and Peachy Melba crept forward, they suddenly heard a very loud grunting noise, followed by the sound of a massive gust of wind whistling across the garden.

Ugenia spun round. To her surprise, there, across the lawn, was the most humongous, ginormous man Ugenia had ever seen in her life. He was curled up, fast asleep, under the shade of a weeping willow.

'We really have to be quiet, Peachy!'

20

whispered Ugenia, suddenly realizing that that wouldn't be a problem for Peachy, who hadn't uttered a single word since she'd met her. 'I just need to get the ball and we have to get out of here without waking the angry giant. Then he won't be any the wiser, right?'

Peachy Melba still said nothing but she gave a very, very scared, trembling smile.

Ugenia approached the broken window. It was going to be impossible to climb through it with all the splintered glass, but next to it was a tiny little window that had been left slightly ajar.

'Oh dear, I am way too big to get through that,' Ugenia said. 'How on earth am I going to get Trevor's football back? A promise is a promise, right?' Ugenia looked

down at little Peachy Melba, not expecting
any answer from Trevor's little sister, who
was staring back up at her. Then, suddenly,
like a thunderbolt of lightning, Ugenia had
a brainwave . . .

'Incredible! You do it!
Peachy, you're small
enough to climb
through the window!'
announced Ugenia,
offering Peachy a
leg-up.

Peachy looked
at her in terror. She
hesitated for a moment, then finally
put her foot in Ugenia's hands and Ugenia
lifted her up towards the open window.
'Now, be really careful you don't leave any

trace behind – we don't want the giant to know we've been here,' whispered Ugenia.

Peachy Melba, as quiet as a mouse, wriggled through the little window and climbed down into the house. The angry giant continued to sleep undisturbed, snoring under the weeping-willow tree.

Ugenia held her breath as she watched Peachy Melba take off her tiny white shoes and place them on the floor before tiptoeing through the kitchen towards the table, where the red leather football sat in the huge pot of mashed potato.

It looked as though Peachy Melba was going to reach for the football, but instead she dipped her hand into the mashed potato, licked her fingers and smiled.

'Peachy, don't touch that!' whispered

Ugenia, as loud as she possibly could. 'We don't want to make the giant even more angry!'

But Peachy Melba continued to scoop the mashed potato into her mouth even more vigorously, completely ignoring Ugenia. Then she took another scoop, and another. In fact, the huge pot of mash was disappearing as fast as you could say, 'Peachy Melba, please don't do that!'

Before Ugenia could call out to Peachy again, she suddenly heard a mighty groan that sounded like a steam train pulling into a station. The angry giant was waking up. Ugenia began to panic. 'Peachy, get out of there, quickly! He's coming! You've eaten all his lunch, he'll be hungry! Now he's going to eat us!'

Peachy wiped the mashed potato from her mouth and began to tremble. She grabbed the red leather football and quickly climbed back up through the tiny window, leaping straight on to Ugenia's back and wrapping her arms around her neck

Ugenia held on tight to Peachy's legs and quickly sped across the beautifully manicured lawn, past the weeping willow and the angry giant, giving Peachy the fastest piggyback in the history of Boxmore.

The angry giant began to stir and growled, 'Who's there?' Then suddenly he was charging through the garden, past the rambling bushes and multicoloured roses, flattening the gardenias, golden dewdrops and honeysuckle, and heading straight towards Ugenia and Peachy Melba.

Frantically Ugenia ran towards the high red-brick walls and climbed up the magnolia tree, still with Peachy on her back, before placing Peachy on a branch.

Peachy Melba trembled among the petals as they tried to hide from the angry giant, who was pacing around the garden directly below them. He muttered something angrily and then marched off back towards the house.

'Come on, Peachy, this is our chance to escape!' whispered Ugenia, trying to take the red leather football from Peachy to throw back over the fence into Granny Betty's garden. But Peachy Melba was frozen to the branch with the ball. She said nothing and didn't move.

'Come on, Peachy, we have to go before he comes back,' said Ugenia, staring at Peachy Melba's orange socks. Suddenly Ugenia had a horrible thought. 'Peachy Melba, where are your shoes?'

But there wasn't time for Peachy to answer her. Suddenly the angry giant came charging out of the house, roaring, 'Who's eaten all my mashed potato? And who do these belong to?' The angry giant looked very, very angry and was holding out a tiny pair of white shoes

as he paced the garden below them.

Peachy Melba began to tremble. She trembled so much that the magnolia tree began to shake its petals, which fell like snow all over the angry giant. The angry giant looked up, even more angrily. Peachy Melba and Ugenia froze. Then suddenly Peachy Melba opened her mouth and screamed the loudest scream you've ever heard.

'DON'T TOUCH MY SHOES!' she shouted as she leaped out of the magnolia tree on to the angry giant's back and began pulling his hair.

'Get off, get off me!' yelped the angry giant, who tumbled to the ground on his knees and began sobbing uncontrollably.

Ugenia quickly jumped down on to the

ground. 'Peachy! Peachy, stop it!' she cried, pulling the little girl off the angry giant's back as she grabbed his nose and tried to bite his right ear.

The angry giant cried like a baby as little Peachy Melba glared at him with rage and snatched back her tiny white shoes.

'Please don't hurt me!' he whimpered.

Ugenia stared in disbelief. He wasn't the evil monster who ate children that Mrs Wisteria had talked about. He seemed more afraid than angry.

'I'm so sorry, we didn't mean to frighten you,' said Ugenia. 'We were just trying to get our football back and we panicked because we thought you were an angry giant trying to eat us.'

The angry giant looked up, surprised,

and stopped crying. 'Eat you? I know I come across as a bit scary but I'd never do anything like that. I'm actually a little bit shy,' explained the not-so-angry giant. 'I find it difficult to speak to new people. It's kind of lonely actually.'

'Well, I think we can fix that,' said Ugenia. 'What shall we call you to start with?'

'My name is Julius,' smiled Julius, when suddenly there was a loud bang at the garden door.

It was Granny Betty, Mrs Wisteria, Crazy Trevor and his neighbour Spike.

'Open the door, you beast!' shouted Mrs Wisteria.

'I'll give you a karate chop if you've hurt Ugenia,' shrieked Granny Betty.

'Don't hurt my sister!' yelled Crazy Trevor.

'I want my ball back,' growled Spike.

Ugenia opened the large wooden door.

'Ugenia, are you all right?' cried Granny Betty. 'We were all so worried! I called Peachy's brother, Trevor, to help.'

'Gran, we're just fine,' beamed Ugenia. 'Meet Julius, the lonely giant,' she said as Julius stepped forward and held out his hand.

'A lonely giant! I had no idea,' said Granny Betty.

'Oh, you poor thing!' added Mrs Wisteria.

'That's a bit sad, innit?' said Spike.

'Er . . . yeah,' said Trevor.

How can we make this better? thought Ugenia as she stared at the lonely giant, the leather football and all the neighbours standing together. Then Ugenia had a brainwave. 'Ingenious!' she cried. 'A game

of footy! And Julius, as you're so tall, you're in goal!'

So Granny Betty, Mrs Wisteria, Spike, Crazy Trevor, Peachy Melba, Ugenia and the not-so-lonely giant began a furious game of karate-chop football with lots of shirt-pulling, vigorous tackling and fake-injury diving.

After forty minutes they all stopped for a break and refreshments.

'Phew, I'm knackered,' said Granny Betty. 'Still, I'm glad it's all worked out!'

'Yes, what fun!' smiled Mrs Wisteria as she pulled her bun loose and let her hair down. 'Everyone behaved beautifully, no one's angry or the slightest bit tricky.'

Trevor and Spike sucked on their oranges and gulped down tarberry juice as they

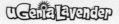

stared curiously at Peachy Melba and
Ugenia.

'Er, Ugenia, Peachy? Why is there
mashed potato on my football?' said Spike.

'And why does Julius have bite marks on
his ear?' said Crazy Trevor.

Peachy Melba and Ugenia both said
nothing and gave very timid smiles.

uGenia Lavender

Big News!

Hi, guys

Well, that certainly was an eye-opener, wasn't it? We had such a great game of football. Crazy Trevor and Spike ended up going home with black eyes after Mrs Wisteria accidentally tackled them. Still, they got the

lovely football back in the end.
And I got two new friends – Julius
and Peachy. And my gran got a
new neighbour, who isn't angry
after all. Also, I reckon that Mrs
Wisteria is all right, once she lets
her hair down a bit. Anyway,
I'm off to the Dinosaur Museum
now. I might ask Peachy to come.
Actually, on second thoughts,
maybe not. She could get a bit
tricky. Anyway, gotta run – I've
got a serious adventure coming up.
It's gonna scare the pants off you!

Big XO
Ugenia Lavender XX

Ingenious Top Tip

Everybody needs somebody

Look how lonely Julius was
without any friends or neighbours.
And now he's got all of us in
his life he's not afraid any more
and is much happier.

uGenia Lavender

and the Beautiful Bloodsucker

It was a cold Friday night and the rain lashed at the window as if it was trying to make a point.
Ugenia was curled up cosily on the sofa with her dog, Misfit, watching her favourite

action hero, Hunk Roberts, in the movie
Jamira Vampira the Black Widow Killer.

Jamira Vampira was a beautiful vampire
who had trapped her many previous
husbands in a ginormous spider's web
before sucking the life out of them. She
had long, dark shiny hair, the blackest of
eyes and pouting red lips. She also had very
long, very sharp teeth and was wearing
a red velvet dress and a long black cape.
Hunk Roberts was going to find it very
hard to resist her evil charms. Would she
manage to suck the hero's blood so she
could live forever?

Ugenia giggled nervously as she hid
behind a cushion. Then she stood up and
popped two cheesy puff crisps in her mouth
as ferocious fangs before creeping over to

her father, who was engrossed in scribbling some notes in the armchair.

'I vant to drink your blood!' growled Ugenia as she loomed over him.

'Do you mind . . . can't you see I'm busy?' snapped Professor Edward Lavender.

'Just bend ze neck to the right slightly.'

'Shh, Ugenia,' sighed Professor Lavender.

'You look so good and I'm so thirsty,' giggled Ugenia.

'Ugenia, that's enough, I've got work to do.'

'All right, all right. Can't you take a joke?!' huffed Ugenia.

'I've no time for jokes this evening. Anyway, you shouldn't be watching that sort of movie – it's far too scary for a girl your age!'

'No it's not, Dad – I don't get scared. Besides, I've seen it loads of times, and Hunk saves the day in the end anyway! It's only a movie, Dad, DUH! Vampires aren't real!'

'Well, actually that's not entirely true,' said Professor Lavender, looking up. 'A type of vampire called a Draclasaurus rex was reportedly found on the Pacific island where the Hadoo Hanuka Hoola Hoola tribe originated many thousands of years ago.' Knitting his eyebrows back together, he continued writing his notes.

'Yeah, right, Dad.' Ugenia laughed.

'I know you're a dinosaur professor and specialist in pretty much everything . . . but AS IF!' And, turning back to the movie, Ugenia was glued to the TV as she watched Jamira Vampira chase Hunk Roberts around the castle.

☆

At the end of the movie Ugenia wrapped the tablecloth around her shoulders as a pretend cape, then ran upstairs to her

43

parents' bedroom, where her mother, Pandora, was busy folding clothes.

'I'm going to suck your blood,' announced Ugenia as she jumped on to the bed and leaped on her.

'Not now, Ugenia, can't you see I'm busy packing . . .' said Pandora, shrugging Ugenia off her shoulders.

'You're always busy!' moaned Ugenia.

All the family was off tomorrow, accompanying Professor Lavender to a special convention to celebrate the work of scientists and consultants (like Professor Lavender) around the world. Ugenia's mother had decided that they should take more interest in her husband's job.

Ugenia was rather bored by the whole idea, but she didn't have much choice in the matter. Still, she was allowed to take Misfit and her best friend, Rudy, with her for company. (It was perfect timing as Rudy's parents were going to visit family in a very small house in Birmingham.)

'Remember that we have a big day tomorrow, Ugenia, so I want you to be on your best behaviour,' Pandora said. 'No funny business, young lady.'

'Injustice!' said Ugenia, before stomping off to bed in a huff.

☆

The next day, the Lavender household was a hive of activity.

Professor Lavender spent the morning busy packing the car with his research materials so that he could show the other

scientists his ideas. Pandora Lavender was busy packing a lunch for the long drive – it was a four-hour car journey to Chumley Castle in Forchester.

Ugenia had already packed her luminous rucksack with her essential items: one torch she'd received for her birthday; one notebook – especially for writing her Big News! Diary; one rope she'd found in her great-grandfather's shed, which she thought may come in handy; one pot of silver nail varnish and one pair of tiger earrings in case any glamour was needed. She and Misfit were ready to go . . .

☆

At midday the Lavenders picked up Rudy in their little Mini and headed up the M678 towards Forchester.

One hour later Ugenia and Rudy were fast asleep and Misfit was dribbling contentedly on Pandora's lap.

Three hours later the Lavenders were driving through thick countryside. Ugenia woke up bursting for a wee. 'Are we nearly there yet?'

'Nearly,' said Professor Lavender, who was actually slightly lost but didn't quite want to admit it.

'Are you lost?' asked Pandora.

'Of course not!' said Professor Lavender as he pulled over to the side of the road to check the map.

Ugenia, Rudy, Pandora and Misfit got out of the car and wandered up the grassy bank where they discreetly hid behind a bush as they all took a very long wee . . .

'I know where we are,' called Professor Lavender. 'It's just five minutes up the road!'

☆

ONE HOUR LATER (it was now five o'clock and beginning to get dark) they found themselves driving very slowly down a narrow country lane, approaching some big iron gates. There was a big sign on them:

WELCOME TO
CHUMLEY CASTLE
I'd turn back it I were you.

'OH MY GOD, A CASTLE!' shrieked Rudy excitedly as the gates drew back to let them through. But Ugenia was more interested in the tiny, scruffy writing at the bottom of the sign. It was so small that she could barely read it. It said: I'd turn back if I were you!

'Did you see that?!' said Ugenia.

'See what?' said Rudy, who was too busy, along with her parents, staring up at the tall trees that lined the long drive. It was a beautiful sight as the trees were covered in biscuit-coloured leaves with a slight frost that glistened like icing sugar.

Ugenia was just about to tell them what she'd read when, suddenly, there in front of them, was the biggest castle she had ever seen. (In fact, Ugenia had never even seen a castle in real life before.) It was made of large grey stones and looked to have five

whole floors and too many windows to count. It was also very old and creepy.

As they parked the car and unloaded the boot, Ugenia stared up at the top of the house, where a man was staring out from behind a curtain at a window. As soon as he caught her watching him he quickly hid.

'Did you see that?' said Ugenia.

'See what?' asked Rudy.

But before Ugenia had time to explain, they were marching up to the house and Professor Lavender was knocking on the large black door.

'Dad, I think this place is creepy,' said Ugenia.

'It's just old, you're going to love it once you meet everyone!' said Professor Lavender as the door gave a creak and swung open . . .

There in front of them was a very tall man with a turban on his head, wearing a tuxedo, shiny black shoes and a tailcoat.

'Welcome . . . sir, madame,' said the man, taking a very deep bow.

'May I introduce Mohammed Ekba,' said Professor Lavender. 'He is the head butler to the Contessa of Ambrosia. I've known him for years – ever since I did some research for her project on Wala-wala-mandu-kat Island.'

'A Contessa and a butler! How fabulous!' shrieked Rudy, jumping up and clapping his hands.

Ugenia groaned and rolled her eyes.

Pandora nudged her. 'Ugenia, we must be on our best behaviour. The Contessa is an old friend of your dad's and has paid for much of the archaeological research he did when we used to travel a lot.'

'Dinner will be at seven in the dining room,' announced Mohammed Ekba. 'The Contessa will be expecting you. Follow me and I'll show you to your rooms.'

The Lavenders followed Mohammed Ekba through the long winding corridors before entering a large hall which had a huge staircase with a dusty red carpet that swept down the middle of it. Ugenia stared at the gigantic black crystal chandelier hanging from the ceiling and noticed a large cobweb dangling from it, right above her head.

They had to walk up four flights of stairs until they finally got to where they were going.

'This is your room,' said Mohammed to Professor and Pandora Lavender, 'and the children will be across the hall.'

Mohammed Ekba ushered Ugenia and Rudy, followed by Misfit, into a large

room a little bit further down the corridor from Ugenia's parents.

The room had wooden panels and was dimly lit. On one of the walls there was a full-length portrait of a beautiful woman with long black hair, a black velvet dress and huge eyes that looked like they were watching you.

The two four-poster beds with heavy green curtains were the biggest beds Ugenia had ever seen in her life.

Rudy shrieked with excitement and threw himself on to one of them. 'It's just like a princess's bed!'

Mohammed Ekba frowned and spoke

sternly. 'I must remind you that the Contessa barely tolerates children in her house. They are rarely seen and definitely not heard.'

Rudy looked at Ugenia; Ugenia looked at Rudy. They both held their breath and as soon as Mohammed Ekba shut the door they burst out laughing.

'This place is fantastic. I wish I could live here,' said Rudy.

'Well, I don't like it,' said Ugenia as she looked out of the diamond-shaped leaded windows on to the grounds in the darkness.

The sun had just sunk into a large lake in the distance as the full moon took residence in the sky, glowing proudly.

'I don't know why, but this whole place is giving me the creeps,' said Ugenia as Misfit

crept under the bed, growling nervously.
'Look – even Misfit doesn't like it.'

'Well, it's only for one night. Let's just
make the most of it,' said Rudy.

☆

Ugenia and Rudy spent the next hour and
a half playing cards before getting ready for
dinner. Rudy put on his eldest brother's best

suit – with sleeves
that were too long
for him.

Ugenia had a
brand-new dress
made from green-
and-blue-tartan satin
taffeta that her mother
had bought especially
for the occasion.

Ugenia put on the dress, but it felt very uncomfortable so she decided to keep her jeans and her big boots on underneath it. Besides, no one would notice. She also put on her tiger earrings for extra glamour.

At five to seven, Ugenia and Rudy left Misfit under the bed quivering and knocked on Pandora and Edward Lavender's door.

Professor Lavender was wearing his best purple suit that he had worn on his wedding day ten years ago.

'Look, it still fits!' said Edward proudly, although it was a little bit tight around his belly. Pandora Lavender was wearing a new mauve floral dress she had bought especially.

Rudy and the Lavender family walked proudly together down the four flights of stairs, through the hall under the black crystal chandelicr with the large cobweb and into the huge dining room.

The dining room had dark red walls (even the ceiling was red) and there was a long table with about twenty people sitting around it all chatting and guzzling wine.

There were mountains of food on the

table – chickens, hams, a roasted stuffed pig, grapes, olives, cheese, potatoes, peaches and long loaves of bread. Ugenia stared at it all in disbelief – she had never seen anything quite like it in her life . . . and she also noticed that everything looked a little bit dusty.

Eeewh – more cobwebs, thought Ugenia. It certainly didn't look as clean as her house in Cromer Road, that's for sure.

Ugenia was ushered to her seat in the middle of the table by Mohammed Ekba. Rudy was sitting opposite her mother, while her father was sitting at the head of the table next to an empty golden throne.

There was a woman in golden robes sitting next to Ugenia. She had little round glasses and long brown hair and her nameplate on the table said 'Sheba

Goldsmith'. She sat in silence and didn't acknowledge Ugenia at all. Ugenia looked round and realized that people were just talking at each other but no one was really listening.

Then, suddenly, Mohammed Ekba rang a bell. 'Ladies and gentlemen, can I have your attention. Please welcome your hostess, the Contessa of Ambrosia.'

Everyone around the table stood up as the dining-room door opened and a beautiful woman with long black silky hair, huge dark eyes and a black velvet dress glided into the room.

'Good evening, you may sit,' said the Contessa, smiling as she took her seat on the golden throne next to Professor Lavender – then everyone around the table sat back down.

'Thank you all for coming tonight,' she announced. 'I'm sorry my husband couldn't be here but he sends his apologies. In the meantime, I would like to explain why you are here. Tonight I will be offering someone funding to set up their very own PERSONAL research project.'

There was a murmur of excitement from the room.

'And there is no point in any of you trying to suck up to me as I have already chosen my two semi-finalists,' cackled the Contessa.

Ugenia stared cautiously at her as she threw back her head and laughed. There was something very familiar about the Contessa and then, suddenly, Ugenia clicked where she'd seen her before – she was in the painting in the bedroom, thought Ugenia.

The Contessa continued. 'The person will come and act as my new personal head researcher. So my two semi-finalists are . . . Doctor Archibald Lecter from the Science University in Oxford for his findings on 'Why does blood look blue in veins?' and secondly Professor Edward Lavender from the Dinosaur Museum in Boxmore for his work on finding the first fossilized Vampasaurus rex tooth.

The crowd applauded.

'Mohammed will announce the winner
at breakfast tomorrow before you leave. Let
the best man win!' she said as she stroked
her long red fingernail across Professor
Lavender's shoulder.

Don't touch my dad, thought Ugenia as
she stared even harder at the Contessa. I
don't trust you.

'Let dinner
commence,' announced
the Contessa as she
picked up a huge juicy
leg of lamb and took a
big bite.

Everyone in the room
began to tuck into the mountains of food,
guzzle more wine and say flattering things
to the Contessa.

'You're such an inspiration to us all,' said Archibald Lecter.

'You've been so generous,' said Professor Lavender.

Ugenia watched the Contessa talking intently to her father and Archibald Lecter.

Everyone was enjoying themselves, all except for Ugenia, who felt extremely uncomfortable and stared at the Contessa suspiciously.

Ugenia tried to get Rudy's attention . . .

'Rudy!' cried Ugenia. But the table was too wide for him to hear her.

So Ugenia pretended to drop her napkin on the floor. As she bent down to pick it up, she slipped down from her chair. When no one was looking she crawled under the table towards Rudy's feet and gave his trouser leg a tug.

Rudy peered under the table. 'What are you doing, Ugenia?'

'We need to have a meeting right now,' said Ugenia urgently.

Rudy slipped under the table. 'What is it?'

'I have a funny feeling,' said Ugenia. 'It's about the Contessa – she can't be trusted.'

'What do you mean? She's lovely and so beautiful. What makes you think that?' said Rudy.

'I don't know exactly,' Ugenia hissed

back. 'I just don't like her, it's my intuition.'

'What's "intuition"?' asked Rudy.

'I heard Hunk Roberts say it in one of his movies . . . it's when you get a funny feeling about something,' said Ugenia. 'You can't explain it but you have to listen to it. Oh, and girls get it stronger than boys, apparently.'

'That's so not fair. I want intuition too,' said Rudy.

'Rudy, life's not fair. Now, look, just follow me,' said Ugenia in her best Hunk Roberts voice.

And before he had time to say any more, Ugenia was crawling out from under the dining-room table. Rudy followed closely until their noses hit a shiny pair of black shoes.

'What are you doing?' said Mohammed
Ekba.

'Erm, we're just going to bed! We're really
tired because we're children!' said Ugenia
with her best innocent smile as she stood up
and straightened out her taffeta dress.

'Very well . . . but go straight to your
rooms,' said Mohammed Ekba. 'I shall
confirm this with your parents . . . and get
them to come up shortly to check on you.'

'Yes, of course,' said Rudy and Ugenia
in unison as they began to walk back up
the staircase.

'Where are we going?' asked Rudy
as they continued to climb right past the
fourth floor, where their bedroom was.

'We're going to the top of the house,'
said Ugenia. 'I didn't get a chance to tell

you before, but I saw someone when we first arrived, staring down at me from one of the windows. It was really weird . . . my intuition tells me we are going to find something ugly about the beautiful Contessa.'

It was extremely dark as Rudy and Ugenia reached the fifth floor, as there was only the glow of tiny candles to light the way. Slowly they crept down the corridor,

staring at the many paintings hanging on the walls. They were all portraits of men, and beneath each one sat a brass plate, engraved with a name and date.

'They all look so pale and tired,' said Ugenia as she looked at a portrait of a balding man with a black moustache and grey skin whose nameplate said Randolf King, 1902. Then there was another of a man with grey hair and silver eyes – Clifton Helsing, 2007.

'I wonder who they are and what the dates mean,' said Rudy. 'Some of them are over a hundred years old!'

Before Ugenia had time to think of an answer, they suddenly heard the staircase creaking. Someone was coming.

Ugenia and Rudy quickly dashed into a tiny dark alcove in the wall and hid. They held their breath as they watched the

Contessa of Ambrosia sweep right past them
and down to the end of the corridor before
turning through a red door and closing it
firmly behind her.

'Come on, we have to follow her,' said
Ugenia.

Ugenia and Rudy tiptoed towards
the red door. Ugenia peered through the
keyhole and could just make out the edge of
a table with some tubes and pipes. She put
her ear to the door and began to listen . . .

'What's wrong with you, Jeffrey, you
stupid imbecile . . . ?!' shouted the Contessa.

'Look, I am trying, but I'm just so
drained, you're sucking the life out of me!'
a man's voice whimpered back.

'Well, I've just about had enough
of you . . . remember YOU ARE

REPLACEABLE!' screamed the Contessa as she headed back towards the door.

Ugenia and Rudy quickly hid back in the alcove as the Contessa flung back the door and stormed down the corridor.

'Ooh my goodness . . . how can someone so beautiful be so vile?' whispered Rudy. 'And who do you think Jeffrey is?'

'Whoever he is, he doesn't sound very happy,' Ugenia whispered back. 'He's probably the one who was hiding at the window when I first arrived. I wonder if he's OK.'

'Ugenia, we'd better be getting back. Your mum is bound to be checking up on us any minute,' said Rudy urgently.

And so Ugenia and Rudy quickly hurried back down the stairs to their bedroom.

Misfit was still shaking nervously under the bed, but he wagged his tail as he was so glad to see them. Ugenia and Rudy quickly brushed their teeth. Ugenia then threw on her Hunk Roberts pyjamas and they both jumped into their beds.

Sure enough, a few minutes later Pandora and Edward Lavender poked their heads around the door.

'Well done, Ugenia and Rudy, you really have behaved impeccably tonight!' said Pandora.

'Thanks, Mum, no problem,' said Ugenia.

'Goodnight,' said Pandora.

'Goodnight,' said Rudy.

'Just one question . . .' asked Ugenia. 'Do you know who Jeffrey is?'

'Jeffrey – I believe is the Contessa's husband,' said Professor Lavender.

'What's he like?' asked Ugenia.

'I've never actually met him,' Professor Lavender answered. 'Why do you ask?'

'Oooh, nothing. Just heard someone say his name, that's all. Night, Dad,' replied Ugenia.

'Night night, sleep tight. Tomorrow's a big day. You never know, I might get chosen by the Contessa to work personally for her! Won't that make you proud?' said Professor Lavender excitedly as he turned off the light.

As soon as he closed the door, Ugenia switched on the light.

'Jeffrey is the Contessa's husband!' she hissed to Rudy. 'And she's keeping him locked up in the top room. And he says she's sucking the life out of him. Rudy, what is the Contessa doing to her husband exactly to suck the life out of him? Rudy? Rudy?'

But Rudy gave no reply except for a very loud snore.

Ugenia felt very anxious. As she looked at the portrait of the Contessa, the eyes seemed to stare back at her. That woman feels so familiar and yet I can't place her. I feel like I've met her before, Ugenia thought. She couldn't sleep as her mind kept on thinking about everything she had seen and heard that day, so she decided to pull out her notebook and pen.

She began to scribble notes . . . a bit like her dad when he was trying to figure something out. Ugenia wrote:

Weird creepy things I've seen and heard

1. Sign: I'd turn back if I were you.
2. Lots of creepy pictures of pale men with names and dates.
3. Possibly Jeffrey, the Contessa's husband, hiding up at the window (when I first arrived).
4. The Contessa is sucking the life out of the REPLACEABLE Jeffrey . . .
5. 'Mohammed will announce the winner at breakfast tomorrow' – quote from Contessa.

Ugenia stared at her notes. It was all too complicated, she couldn't figure it out.

Ugenia just felt scared. All she could hear was deadly silence except for a few creaks from the corridor as the rest of the castle slept soundly.

Ugenia stared down at her Hunk Roberts pyjamas . . . and thought of how she wished she was back at home on her safe, cosy sofa watching a Hunk Roberts movie, like the one when he'd wrestled with Jamira Vampira, the Bloodsucking Vampire.

Then Ugenia stared at the portrait of the beautiful Contessa, who was still staring straight back at her.

Then suddenly, like a thunderbolt of lightning, Ugenia had a brainwave . . .

'Incredible!' THE CONTESSA IS A VAMPIRE, SHE'S A BLOODSUCKER!' shrieked Ugenia as she leaped across the room on to Rudy's bed.

'Wake up, Rudy. The Contessa is sucking the life out of Jeffrey!'

'What are you talking about?' said Rudy, rubbing his eyes.

'I reckon she sucked the life out of all those men in the paintings too. That's why they look so grey!'

'How can someone so beautiful on the outside be so evil? She's too beautiful to be a vampire bloodsucker, isn't she?'

'No, Rudy. She is a beautiful bloodsucker! Trust me – it's my intuition! Just like Jamira Vampira in the Hunk Roberts movie. And my dad did say vampires do exist, right?'

'Look, don't worry . . . we can sort this out tomorrow at breakfast when she chooses her new researcher,' said Rudy, who just wanted to get back to sleep.

'No, Rudy, don't you see, she's not choosing a new researcher, she is choosing a new husband to drain tomorrow at breakfast and I reckon she's after my dad! We have to stop her!'

'OK, calm down,' said Rudy, who sat up and scratched his head.

'I guess it's time for a mission impossible called "Stop, you beautiful bloodsucker!" And you need the best person for the job, so that would be me,' yawned Rudy with a smile. 'But I'm afraid I don't have my vision board.'

'We'll manage!' said Ugenia excitedly.

Ugenia and Rudy made a simple list of all the things they had seen in movies that they knew stopped vampires.

1. GARLIC - SPIKE HER BREAKFAST? GET FROM KITCHEN.

2. MIRRORS - VAMPIRES HATE REFLECTION. GET HAND MIRROR FROM BATHROOM.

3. SUNLIGHT - VAMPIRES MELT IN THE SUN.

4. WATER - POSSIBLY - IT DEFINITELY WORKS ON WITCHES - SEEN IN MOVIE.

5. STEAK THROUGH THE HEART - HAVEN'T ACTUALLY SEEN BUT CRAZY TREVOR TALKED ABOUT IT ONCE.

6. HOLD A CROSS TO THEM - PLEASE NOTE: VAMPIRES SLEEP DURING MORNING, SO BEST TIME TO STRIKE.

Rudy and Ugenia crept down the stairs to the castle kitchen to find what they needed. They would put their plan into operation first thing next morning, when the beautiful bloodsucking vampire was still sleeping.

☆

At six o'clock in the morning Ugenia got

up, thanks to her new watch that had an alarm that beeped. She put everything they needed into her luminous yellow rucksack. Holding a bucket of water as a last-resort

measure for safety, Rudy and Ugenia
(who was still wearing her Hunk Roberts
pyjamas) crept out of the bedroom up the
flight of stairs to the next floor.

They tiptoed down the corridor past the
creepy portraits. It was just getting light
and the sun was about to come up as they
approached the red door.

'I reckon this is where her coffin is
kept . . .' whispered Ugenia. 'We have to
be careful – this is life or death, Rudy. She
might turn on us, but we have to save
my dad!'

Slowly Ugenia turned the door handle
and crept inside the room . . . she could
hear snoring and heavy breathing. It was
still fairly dark, so it was hard for Ugenia to
see exactly what was there.

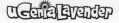

She sprinkled some finely chopped cloves of garlic over the dark, sleeping figure and held a hand mirror ready. She then gave Rudy the signal to creep over to the window and swish back the curtains to let the sunlight in.

Suddenly, as the sunlight leaped into the room, the sleeping Contessa, who was lying in bed next to a snoring Jeffrey, opened her eyes and screamed.

Ugenia quickly held the mirror to the Contessa's face. The Contessa looked in the mirror and screamed louder. 'Aaaah, I look awful.' She sat up with her hair sticking out and hissed, 'What are you doing in MY BEDROOM?'

'Quick, Rudy, the steak! We have no time to lose,' shrieked Ugenia.

Rudy quickly slapped the piece of raw steak they had stolen from the fridge downstairs on to the Contessa's chest. She was wearing a white nightie.

'What on earth is going on?' mumbled Jeffrey, who was now beginning to wake from his deep sleep.

'In the name of truth, you must stop, you bloodsucking vampire!' shouted Ugenia as she held up two chopsticks crossed together.

'It's not working, Rudy – we must use the last resort.' Ugenia quickly grabbed the bucket of water beside the bed and threw it over the Contessa.

Suddenly Jeffrey also sat up, rubbed his eyes in disbelief and stared at the drenched Contessa, who was fuming with anger as she leaped out of bed and ran to the bathroom bawling, 'Do something, Jeffrey, you know I can't stand children!'

Jeffrey burst out laughing. 'Good morning,' he said, 'and who are you?'

'My name is Ugenia Lavender. This is

Rudy. We have come to stop her sucking the life out of you AND my dad, Professor Lavender, who is next on her list.'

'Well, she certainly is doing that! But why all the water and garlic and steak?' laughed Jeffrey.

'It's the only way to stop a vampire sucking your blood,' said Rudy.

'Ah,' said Jeffrey. 'I see. But there's been a mistake. You're right, she is sucking the life out of me – being married *and* working for the Contessa is very tiring. She can be so demanding – but it's not my blood she's after; it's my work, my research. Being her husband and working for her personally is too much – it's just so full on. That's why she's looking for a new personal researcher.'

'But what about the paintings of the

other men she has killed that are hanging on the walls?' said Ugenia. 'They even have their names and dates.'

'Ah.' Jeffrey nodded. 'Those are the scientists who have received special awards from the Contessa's family – the trust fund has been going for hundreds of years.'

'Ooops!' said Ugenia. 'I guess I've made a huge mistake – she's not a beautiful bloodsucking vampire after all.'

Jeffrey laughed. 'Well, maybe not a bloodsucker – more an emotional vampire who can be a bit draining! Thanks for trying to help, but I think it's best if you go back down to your parents. I shall talk to the Contessa and get her to forget all about this little misunderstanding.'

Ugenia and Rudy thought this was a

good idea and quickly left the room before
the Contessa got back from the bathroom.
They had just got back to their bedroom
and were getting ready for breakfast when
Professor Lavender and Pandora popped
their heads round the door.

'Morning, everything all right?' said
Pandora.

'Fine,' smiled Ugenia sweetly.

'Well, good, pack your things – we're
leaving,' said her mum. 'You'll have
breakfast in the car.'

'But what about finding out whether
Dad's going to be the Contessa's personal
researcher?' said Ugenia.

'Ah, well, there's been a change of heart,'
said Professor Lavender. 'Last night the
Contessa told me exactly what is required

from the new job, and it sounded very demanding. Your mother and I have been talking and we feel we're busy enough as it is. I suddenly realized I'd rather spend time with my lovely family,' smiled Professor Lavender. 'Besides, I didn't really want to leave the museum.'

'You get ready to leave and we'll meet downstairs. I'm going to tell the Contessa right now that I don't want to work for her as I'm happy where I am, thank you very much!'

Ugenia smiled with relief. 'Now that's made me proud, Dad. You really are a specialist in pretty much everything, including what makes ME happy!' She hugged her dad.

☆

After they said goodbye to Mohammed Ekba and everyone else in the castle, Edward and Pandora Lavender, Ugenia and Rudy, along with Misfit, got back in the Mini, ready for their journey back to Boxmore.

89

As they drove back down the long drive lined with beautiful trees, something made Ugenia look back up at the castle's top window. There she could see the Contessa peering out from behind the curtain, with Jeffrey lurking just behind her. Ugenia began to think about her muddled intuition. 'The Contessa wasn't a bloodsucking vampire after all,' she murmured.

The Contessa stared back down at Ugenia as if she was reading her mind.

'Or was she?' thought Ugenia as the Contessa gave her a very evil smile . . .

uGenia Lavender

Big News!

Hello

Was she or wasn't she?

I can't decide if it was my mind playing tricks on me.

Although my intuition did get me in a spot of bother, my hunch was sort of correct. Somehow I knew that the Contessa would make my family unhappy if my dad worked for her personally.

Anyway, that's old news . . . I need to tell you something very important. I found out ages ago, but I forgot to tell you as so many other things were happening, plus I didn't quite believe it but there's no denying it now . . . basically, my mother is expecting a baby! I'm going to get a new brother or sister in a few months!

Can you imagine? I'm not sure how I feel about it, but since my mother's stomach is really sticking out and she's eating anything and everything, it's definitely happening. I just hope I'm still important to her, that's all.

Got to go . . . I have homework – boring!

Big XO
Ugenia Lavender XX

Ingenious Top Tip

Happiness is loving what you have

I reckon my dad learned that this weekend . . . he realized that even though the Contessa was offering him his own personal project – which sounded very exciting – he really loved working at the museum and spending more time with his family. That is what makes him happy.

3

UGenia Lavender

and the Temple of Gloom

It was a dark November evening. The wind crashed around like a fiery dragon's breath and rain lashed at the windows. Ugenia was feeling very gloomy – she'd been sent to bed early with no TV, which was a real disaster, because the movie *Killer Onion Savages* was on, starring her favourite all-action superhero, Hunk Roberts.

Ugenia stared out of the window. I hate my life, she thought bitterly as she recalled

what had happened earlier . . .

That afternoon, Rudy and Ugenia had decided to skip class and instead head off to the school field to climb very tall trees. It was the first time ever that Ugenia had missed a lesson on purpose, but she was sure nobody would notice. However, Ugenia was very much mistaken.

They'd only been gone ten minutes when the caretaker, Mr Hector, spotted Ugenia and Rudy sneaking through a hole in the fence leading to the field.

'Gotcha!' he cackled, giving them his most triumphant vinegar smile. In no time at all he had sent them both to the head teacher, Mrs Hyde.

Mrs Hyde called their parents.

Ugenia's parents were very angry.

'How could you?' said Mum.

'We're so disappointed,' said Dad.

'You naughty, naughty girl!' they both said. 'Up to your room and no TV!'

'But the Hunk Roberts movie is on!' protested Ugenia.

'No buts,' said Dad. 'Off you go now!'

'But it's the best one, where he saves the Little Radish People!' protested Ugenia.

'No buts – go to your room!' said Mum.

'I hate my life!' shouted a very stroppy Ugenia. 'And I hate you!'

Ugenia had decided that this was one battle she wasn't going to win, so she

had stomped upstairs to her bedroom in
a mighty huff and slammed her bedroom
door behind her so the whole house
trembled. Then she lay down on her bed in
her favourite Hunk Roberts space pyjamas
and stared at her Hunk Roberts action-hero
wallpaper . . .

Now Ugenia found herself lying on
the bed feeling rather tired from the day's
events. Before she knew it, her eyelids were
getting heavy and she drifted off to sleep.

☆

The next morning Ugenia woke in her
usual Ugenia way. She turned off her alarm
clock (which buzzed like a chainsaw drill)
with a good whack and stretched out her
arms. She leaped out of bed in her Hunk
Roberts action-hero fashion, but to her

surprise she felt weighed down by a heavy, gloomy feeling that seemed to loom over her like a black cloud. Ugenia decided that perhaps she had got out the wrong side of the bed, so decided to start all over again. She climbed back into bed and pulled the covers over her head. Then she closed and reopened her eyes and leaped out of bed the other side.

But to Ugenia's dismay, she felt even more gloomy than before. As she hit the floor, Ugenia felt something very weird underneath her feet. She looked down and, to her surprise, she saw that her snug, cosy bedroom carpet wasn't there. Instead there was a very cold, very hard, stone floor. Stranger still, there seemed to be some sort of gooey slime on it, which smelt a bit like

her mum's strong disinfectant detergent
– Ugenia's mum, Pandora, was very keen
on cleaning.

'Yuck!' said Ugenia. 'I think Mum's been
in extra-cleaning mode again!'

Ugenia wandered sleepily through the
hall and into the bathroom. Was it her
imagination or was the wallpaper missing?
And what was that dark green mould on the
ceiling, dripping with what looked like snot?

Mum and Dad must be decorating again,
thought Ugenia. (Her parents were DIY
fanatics, who could spend a whole weekend
looking round Basehome Superstore.)

As Ugenia peered into the bathroom
mirror, pretending she was in her favourite
toothpaste advert, she spotted something out
of the corner of her eye. She spun round.

There in the bathtub was a very round man wearing a pointy black hat and a black-and-white stripy T-shirt that was far too small for him, so that his pot belly poked out underneath. He had a massive red bag slung across his body.

'Why are you in the bath wearing a red bag?' demanded Ugenia.

'I can't pee if there's a decorator in the bathroom. Get out!'

'I'm not a decorator!' exclaimed the man. 'I'm Theodore the Wizard.' He took a bow and tipped his pointy black hat.

'Yeah, right, whatever!' snapped Ugenia. 'I need my privacy. GET OUT!'

'Oooohh!' said Theodore. 'Who's been sucking on a lemon, Miss Grumpy Groodles! What's with the gloom?'

But before Ugenia could answer, Theodore had hopped out of the bath and gone over to the toilet.

'If you want to lose the gloom,' he grinned, 'then follow me down the WC!'

And with that, he jumped into the toilet and flushed the chain.

'The only way is through and under . . .' Ugenia heard him call as he disappeared down the toilet.

'Was he for real,' Ugenia asked herself, 'or was that my imagination? Maybe I'll just flush and see.' Ugenia dived head first into the toilet, giving it a big flush and holding her nose to avoid any possible poo.

With a massive whoosh, Ugenia found herself sliding down a dark and slippery tunnel. 'Aaaaaaaaaarrrrrrghhhhhhh!' she screamed as she whizzed down forwards, half scared out of her wits and half enjoying the ride.

Then, before she knew it, she had plopped out of the tunnel and found herself on a tatty brown sofa in a dentist's surgery

waiting room.
It was
very dark
and miserable
around her
– the walls were
a peppermint-
green colour
and the room
smelt of vomit.
Ugenia could hear
wailing coming from
outside in the corridor. On the far side of
the room there was a large white door with
the word 'Dentist' on it.

Hmm . . . this doesn't feel very friendly,
thought Ugenia as she stared at someone
hiding behind a very large newspaper.

Ugenia looked at the newspaper headlines facing her:

A GLOOMY RESULT FOR THE NATIONAL FOOTBALL TEAM

MORE DOOM AND GLOOM FOR POP STAR DYLAN COHEN

GLOOMY WEATHER TO CONTINUE – ESPECIALLY DOWN THE WC, WHERE IT WILL BE WET AND COLD!

Hmm . . . well, it certainly is wet and cold down here, thought Ugenia. She was starting to feel gloomier than ever when suddenly she noticed the top of a pointy hat, poking up above the newspaper.

'Hold on a minute!' she gasped. 'Isn't that Theodore?' She leaned forward and

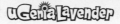

snatched away the newspaper. But to Ugenia's amazement there was no one there . . . just a massive red bag and a green envelope. She opened the envelope and found a letter inside.

Dear Ugenia,
Welcome to the Temple of Gloom.
The only way out is to retrieve
the golden loo-brush.
Big hug
T.W.
PS Through and under.
PPS The red bag might be
useful.

UGENIA opened the red bag and found:
  1 giant roll of toilet paper

1 large pack of
dental floss
1 small silver
hand mirror

The Temple of Gloom sounds pretty horrible, thought Ugenia, but it couldn't get much worse than this gloomy feeling, could it?

Suddenly Ugenia felt quite alone and wished she could be back home in her cosy room, with her cosy carpet, safely tucked up in her cosy bed. But at that second, Ugenia heard a voice from a loudspeaker.

'Please could all visitors fill in the registration form before seeing Mr Myron Molar – the best dentist in the world, thank you very much!'

Ugenia look to her left and noticed that right beside her on the sofa was a clipboard with a registration form. She checked out the form.

QUESTIONNAIRE
Why did you skip class?
How long for?
Did you really think you'd get away with it? Yes/No
Screwdriver or pliers for teeth extraction?

'Injustice!' huffed Ugenia. 'I didn't skip class . . . and what does extraction mean anyway?'

But before she even had the time to fill in the questionnaire, the loudspeaker spoke again. 'Miss Ugenia Lavender, Mr Myron

Molar – best dentist in the world, thank you very much – will see you now.' A door swung open and Mr Molar skidded across the floor on his knees.

'Welcome to my world!' he crooned into a microphone.

Mr Molar was a very short man with a very flat head and a shiny quiff, who clearly enjoyed doing an Elvis impression.

'Come and lie on my big chair,' he sang, guiding Ugenia to a large shiny dentist's chair that was covered with jagged pearls. 'Now, let's look at those little biters of yours.'

Ugenia lay back as Mr Molar inspected her mouth with two large instruments, one to keep her mouth open, the other to prod. 'Just as I thought. Ten minutes of skipping your maths class equals ten teeth to be extracted – that means pulled out,' chuckled the dentist. 'And you thought you'd get away with it, so no anaesthetic!'

'I on't ont at – ees, oh!' squealed Ugenia, meaning, 'I don't want that – please, no!'

'Shush, shush,' hummed Mr Molar, 'this will only take a minute, but I need to find my pliers first – back in a mo.'

Once Mr Molar had left the room, Ugenia leaped out of the chair, burst out through the door and sped down the corridor as fast as her feet would carry her. Suddenly, there in front of her, was a sign with swirling, rusty letters:

THE TEMPLE OF
GLOOM
ENTER AT YOUR
OWN RISK

Ugenia looked over her shoulder.

'Come back, I need those ten teeth!' shouted Mr Molar, charging down the corridor behind her.

'The only way is through and under, right?' she panted to herself.

Ugenia pushed the emerald door open, ran through and slammed it shut behind her. She found herself in a dimly lit tunnel and was starting to feel the heavy, gloomy feeling again, when she heard a boy's voice screaming.

'No, please don't eat me! Really, I'm not that tasty!'

To Ugenia's horror, there in front of her was a large crocodile with her best friend, Rudy, wedged inside its mouth.

'Rudy! How did you get

down here?' Ugenia sprang forward, pretending she wasn't afraid.

'Ugenia!' shrieked Rudy, 'I am SO glad to see you!'

'Don't worry! I'm going to get you out of there!' said Ugenia in her best Hunk Roberts voice.

'Hurry, Ugenia,' pleaded Rudy. 'This croc is sucking on me like an ice pop!'

The crocodile suddenly gave a yelp and Rudy closed his eyes, preparing to be swallowed. But instead of munching on Rudy, tears rolled down the crocodile's face.

'I think this croc is in some sort of pain,' said Ugenia, bending down and taking a closer look in its mouth. 'Insufferable! Vicious toothache! Ingenious! The red bag!'

Quickly Ugenia opened Theodore's red

bag and pulled out the list. She stuck the mirror into the croc's mouth and showed him a reflection of his very rotten tooth. Reaching for the loo paper, she placed it very carefully over the painful tooth so he could bite on it for comfort.

'Thank you!' said the croc, releasing Rudy from his jaws. 'That's so much more comforting than Rudy was.'

Ugenia looked around her, spotting the mountain of supersized caramel fudge wrappers on the ground. 'Maybe you should change your diet,' she said. 'Uncle Harry's friend Oliver knows all about healthy eating. Perhaps you should read one of his books. And perhaps you should lay off little boys like Rudy too.'

'I wasn't trying to EAT him!' the croc

said indignantly. 'I'm a vegetarian!'

At that very second, there was a loud creaking sound behind them. Ugenia, Rudy and the croc turned at the same time and spied a furious Mr Molar, running towards them, brandishing a gigantic pair of pliers.

'Delicious!' said the croc, licking his lips.

'But I thought you were a vegetarian,' said Ugenia.

'I am,' grinned the croc, flushing a fiendish smile, 'but I make a special exception for dentists. Don't you worry – I'll take care of him.'

And so, Ugenia and Rudy sped off ahead, escaping down the tunnel. They'd

only gone a short way when they ran into
a barrier bearing a large sign that said:

DO NOT ENTER
PREPARE TO SINK

'Through and under,' thought Ugenia,
remembering the echo of Theodore's voice.
'Let's do this!' she shouted, limbo-dancing
her body under the barrier.

Rudy followed along behind her and they
soon reached the bank of a murky swamp.

'This can't be right,' said Ugenia, peering
into the distance, where she could see a
little rock that was glowing.

Ugenia squinted. 'It's the golden loo-
brush!' she declared. 'That's exactly what we

need to get out of here! Theodore said so!'

'I wouldn't bother if I were you,' said a very low, sad voice.

Ugenia peered ahead of her. There in the middle of the swamp was a turtle.

'Why not?' she asked. (Ugenia hated it when people told her she couldn't do things, especially when they didn't even know her.)

'Well, I've been here for a very long time,' explained the turtle, 'and I can't manage to reach it.' As he said this, the turtle sank a little.

'Why?' questioned Ugenia.

'I'm just not good enough,' replied the turtle glumly. 'In fact, I'm not really good at anything.' And with that, he sank a little more. 'You see, I'm not strong enough.'

Down he went again. 'This is the Temple

of Gloom and I can't fight it . . . I . . .'

'STOP! Don't say another word!' commanded Ugenia, realizing that every time the turtle said something negative, he sank even more. Then suddenly, like a thunderbolt of lightning, Ugenia had a brainwave. 'Ingenious!' she cried. 'Good thoughts!'

'Er . . . I can't think of anything good,' said the turtle, sinking even lower.

The swamp water was now up to his nose.

'Come on!' pleaded Ugenia. 'You must be able to think of something good.'

The turtle thought for a few seconds. 'There's my mum, I guess,' he said.

'That's good!' urged Ugenia. 'Think some more. What's your favourite food?

Mine is spaghetti hoops.'

The turtle suddenly smiled. 'Mine too!' he replied. 'I love to suck 'em down in one go!'

Ugenia quickly did her best impression of sucking on a spaghetti hoop and the turtle began to giggle.

Ugenia started to laugh, then so did Rudy. Before they knew it, they were all laughing hysterically. And then, to their amazement, the turtle was suddenly floating right on the top of the swamp and drifting towards Ugenia and Rudy.

Without a second thought, Ugenia and Rudy leaped on to his back.

'I hope you don't mind,' said Ugenia, 'but we need a ride.'

'No problem!' The turtle grinned. 'Where are we going?'

'To the golden loo-brush!' declared Ugenia.

But as they approached the golden loo-brush, the turtle seemed to smack into an invisible wall.

'Oh dear,' said the turtle, 'we've hit a portal loo.'

'But we need the golden loo-brush to get home,' insisted Ugenia. 'What are we going to do?' As she pondered this difficult question, Ugenia had another brainwave. 'Totally ingenious!' she cried. 'The dental floss!'

Without hesitation, Ugenia pulled the

dental floss out of the red bag. Making a
lasso, she threw it high into the air. The
dental floss cleared the invisible portal loo,
then looped round the golden loo-brush.
Ugenia gave the floss a swift tug and
the brush flew
straight back
into her
hands. 'Now
what do
I do?'
she
mused.
'Theodore said this
brush would get me out of here.'

Then suddenly there was a loud cracking
sound, as if the walls were about to come
tumbling down and, to Ugenia's horror, th

123

turtle began to sink. 'Quick,' she shouted, 'we must get back to the bank.'

'I can't think good thoughts under pressure!' the turtle gurgled, sinking even further.

'You're not under pressure!' screamed Ugenia, who was now also feeling under pressure as a tidal wave of filthy sludge emerged from the swamp and flooded towards them.

'I'm drowning!' shrieked the turtle. 'What shall we do?'

'Improvisation!' cried Ugenia. 'A loo-brush paddle!'

Ugenia then began paddling furiously with her new golden water paddle, as fast as she possibly could.

'Theodore was right!' she shouted. 'The

only way out is to retrieve the golden loo-brush!'

They sped on, the tidal wave looming above them. Quick as a flash, they reached the bank, and Rudy and Ugenia leaped off the turtle's back. Ugenia grabbed the turtle and stuffed him under her arm before limboing under the barrier with Rudy and sprinting off back down the tunnel. They followed the passage round, turning this way and that until finally they came to a towering cliff-top. Below them was a huge drop down into a deep, dark sewer.

'JUMP!' shouted Ugenia.

Rudy and Ugenia flung themselves over the cliff edge into the sewer and landed with a gigantic splash.

Ugenia felt herself sinking deeper and deeper into the water. She was very scared and was sure she was drowning. She thought of her mum and dad. She would miss them and they would miss her. She wished she could see them and say sorry for skipping school.

Then, just as Ugenia was giving up all hope of ever emerging from this desperate place, she felt herself being pulled up by the back of her pyjamas.

'Thank goodness!' thought Ugenia. 'I'm saved!'

She quickly looked around. 'Ooooh no!' cried Ugenia. There was no Rudy, no

Theodore, no turtle, no croc – just
Mr Molar, who was strapping her tightly
into his dentist's chair with two vicious
steel straps.

'At last I can get those ten teeth of yours!'
cackled Mr Molar. 'Plus two extra for
setting that crocodile on me, you naughty,
naughty girl!'

Mr Molar reached for his drill and lunged
towards her mouth.

Ugenia closed her eyes and screamed as
she heard the dentist's drill, which buzzed
like a chainsaw. Was this the end for her
and her teeth? Ugenia cringed in horror as
she waited for the deadly pain to come, but
then nothing seemed to be happening . . .

Ugenia flinched and opened her eyes to
find herself staring at her Hunk Roberts

wallpaper. She turned off her alarm clock (which buzzed like a chainsaw drill) with a good whack and stretched her arms.

'Thank goodness it was just a dream,' she thought as her feet snuggled into the cosy bedroom carpet. 'None of it really happened.'

She gazed out of the window. The garden was bathed in warm sunshine and she suddenly realized that she didn't feel gloomy any more as she started to get ready for school.

She could hear the postman pushing

some letters into the postbox and the
footsteps of her dad as he picked them up
and went back to the kitchen.

Ugenia looked out of the
window and caught a
glimpse of the back
of the postman. It
looked like he was
wearing a black
pointy hat and he
had a big red bag.

'Don't be silly,' she told herself,
'it's just my imagination.'

Ugenia ran downstairs into the kitchen
and threw her arms round her mum
and dad.

'I'm SO happy to see you!' she laughed.
'And I'm really sorry about yesterday and

I'm ready for school.'

'Oh, don't you remember?' asked her mum.

'Remember what?' said Ugenia blankly.

'There's no school for you this morning,' replied her mum, pointing at a green envelope.

Ugenia opened the envelope and stared at the card inside.

REMINDER
A check-up today has been booked for
MISS UGENIA LAVENDER, with your new
dentist . . .
Mr M. Molar

Big News!

HELLO there!
OK, when you were reading
that story, were you thinking,
What the heck is going on? Is she
for real? Getting flushed down a
toilet – bizarre or what?

Anyway, it was all a dream,
thank goodness! I suppose that's

the beauty and the nightmare of
a dream – anything can happen,
good and bad stuff. Depends what
kind of mood I'm in before I go
to bed. And I was in *such* a bad
mood! Anyway, it's all got much
better, thank goodness! I suppose
I learned a bit of a lesson, blah
blah boring!

Oh, I tell you what I forgot
to mention – when I went to the
dentist (how bizarre was it that he
had the same name as the dentist
in my dream?), he was also slightly
weird. For a moment I was scared
he was going to try and take my

teeth out, but he didn't. He just told me to brush more often and gave me an electric toothbrush – actually extremely important I think if I'm going to either appear in a toothpaste advert (I practise smiling daily) or become extremely famous and have to smile a lot . . . who knows, both might lead to faceache, in which case maybe I won't bother!

Big XO
Ugenia Lavender XX

Ingenious Top Tip

To get off the pity pot, get grateful

I've learned that when everything seems a bit rubbish and I feel gloomy, the way to not sink further into a gloomy hole is to be thankful for stuff – anything – big and little things. That always seems to cheer me up.

Brain
Squeezers

Ugenia's Weird Wordsearch

My life's certainly been a bit, well, weird lately! And I've met a strange selection of creatures and people – can you find them in this wordsearch? The words may be up, down, backwards, forwards or even diagonal!

CROCODILE ~~DENTIST~~ GIANT
~~TURTLE~~ ~~VAMPIRE~~ ~~WIZARD~~

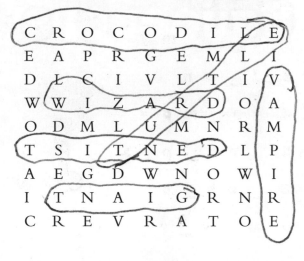

```
C  R  O  C  O  D  I  L  E
E  A  P  R  G  E  M  L  I
D  L  C  I  V  L  T  I  V
W  W  I  Z  A  R  D  O  A
O  D  M  L  U  M  N  R  M
T  S  I  T  N  E  D  L  P
A  E  G  D  W  N  O  W  I
I  T  N  A  I  G  R  N  R
C  R  E  V  R  A  T  O  E
```

Ugenia's Vowels of Gloom

Oh dear! My journey to the Temple of Gloom turned out to be a nightmare. I'm *very* glad I'm not there any more! All the words below are associated with the feeling 'down in the dumps'. Can you fill in the missing vowels – a, e, i, o and u – to complete the words?

1. s **a** d

2. g l **o o** m y

3. d **o** w n

4. g r **u** m p y

5. **u** n h **a** p p y

6. **u** p s **e** t

7. m **i** s **e** r **a** b l **e**

Ugenia's Bloodsucking Word Grid

I'm still feeling a bit 'creeped out' after my experience with the beautiful bloodsucker, the Contessa of Ambrosia. And I know loads about vampires now! How much do you know? Solve the six clues to find something that all vampires hate, which will be revealed in the vertical box!

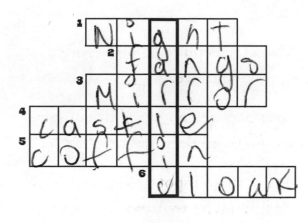

1. Night
2. Fangs
3. Mirror
4. Castle
5. Coffin
6. Cloak

1. Vampires hate daylight, so they only come out at n i g h t.

2. Vampires have two very sharp teeth, which they bite with! What are the teeth called?

3. Vampires can't stand their reflections, so a real vampire will always avoid one of these.

4. A huge, creepy building, where a vampire might live.

5. Cosy beds are no place for vampires -- they prefer to sleep in one of these.

6. How can you spot a vampire? Well, it will usually be wearing a sweeping black c l o a k.

Ugenia's True or False?

How much can you remember about my incredible life? Try my true or false quiz and find out!

1. My groovy grandmother, Granny Betty, is an amazing 101 years old.

■ TRUE ☐ FALSE

2. When me and Peachy Melba accidentally kicked a football into a giant's garden, Peachy went in and found a cooking pot full of sausages.

☐ TRUE ■ FALSE

3. I have a great dog, whose name is Dimwit.

☐ TRUE ■ FALSE

4. Vampires don't like sunlight.
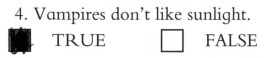 ☑ TRUE ☐ FALSE

5. To get back home from the Temple of Gloom, I had to find a silver loo-brush.
☐ TRUE  ☑ FALSE

6. Mr Molar is a dentist.
☑ TRUE ☐ FALSE

Ugenia's Vowels of Gloom

1. sad
2. gloomy
3. down
4. grumpy
5. unhappy
6. upset
7. miserable

Ugenia's True or False?

1. TRUE
2. FALSE. It was full of mashed potatoes.
3. FALSE. My dog's called Misfit!
4. TRUE
5. FALSE. It was a golden loo-brush.
6. TRUE

Ugenia's Bloodsucking Word Grid

¹n	i	g	h	t		
²f	a	n	g	s		
³m	i	r	r	o	r	
⁴c	a	s	t	l	e	
⁵c	o	f	f	i	n	
⁶c	l	o	a	k		

Ugenia's Weird Wordsearch

```
C R O C O D I L E
E A P R G E M L I
D C I O V L T I Y
WWI Z A R D O A
O D M L U M N R M
T S I N E D L P
A E G D WN OWI
I T N A I G R N R
C R E V R A T O E
```

144

uGenia Lavender
Home Alone

Ugenia Lavender is off on holiday. What's
it like being stranded on a desert island?
Will she get back from holiday in time to
ride the scariest ride ever at the Lunar Park
Funfair? And just how will she get back
to school in one piece? That depends on
what happens when Ugenia is left Home
Alone . . .

uGenia Lavender

The One and Only

Ugenia Lavender has discovered that the planet is fast running out of energy. But luckily she has a plan to save the day. How can she help an alien return to outer space? And what happens when she meets her hero, Hunk Roberts? Does it make up for the fact that Ugenia might no longer be the One and Only?

Collect all 6 uGenia Lavender books!

Geri Halliwell

uGenia Lavender

She's totally ingenious!

Got it! ▰

Geri Halliwell

uGenia Lavender and the Terrible Tiger

Got it! ☐

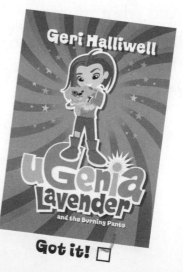

Geri Halliwell

uGenia Lavender and the Burning Pants

Got it! ☐

Geri Halliwell

uGenia Lavender
Home Alone

Got it! ☐

Geri Halliwell

uGenia Lavender
and the Temple of Gloom

Got it!

Geri Halliwell

uGenia Lavender
The One and Only

Got it! ☐

Log on to

ugenialavender

.com

for ingenious fun!

**Enter the world of
Ugenia Lavender and get ready
for a whole lot of fun!**

**You can find out more about the Ugenia
Lavender series plus play ingenious
games, watch fun videos and
download buddy icons and more.**

Collect all six books and get a FREE Ugenia Photo Frame!

Photo frame supplied without Geri's photo

There is a token in each Ugenia Lavender book – collect all six tokens and you can get your very own, totally free UGENIA LAVENDER photo frame!

Send your six tokens, along with your name, address and parent/guardian's signature (you must get your parent/guardian's signature to take part in this offer) to: Ugenia Lavender Photo Frame Offer, Marketing Dept, Macmillan Children's Books, 20 New Wharf Road, London N1 9RR

Terms and conditions: Open to UK and Eire residents only. Purchase of the six Ugenia Lavender books is necessary. Offer not open to those over the age of twelve. Please ask permission of your parent/guardian to enter this offer. One photo frame per entry and per household. Actual photo frame may differ from one shown. No group entries allowed. Photocopied tokens will not be accepted. Photo frames are distributed on a first come, first served basis, while stocks last. No part of the offer is exchangeable for cash or any other offer. The closing date for this offer is 31/01/09. Please allow 28 days for delivery. We will use your data only for the purpose of fulfilling this offer. We will not pass information on to any third parties. All data will be destroyed after the promotion. For full terms and conditions, write to: Ugenia Lavender Photo Frame Offer, Marketing Dept, Macmillan Children's Books, 20 New Wharf Road, London N1 9RR

Ugenia Lavender Photo Frame Offer

Token 5

Collect all six tokens and get your free photo frame

Valid until 31/01/09

A selected list of titles available from Macmillan Children's Books

The prices shown below are correct at the time of going to press. However, Macmillan Publishers reserves the right to show new retail prices on covers, which may differ from those previously advertised.

Geri Halliwell

Ugenia Lavender	978-0-230-70140-3	£6.99
Ugenia Lavender and the Terrible Tiger	978-0-230-70142-7	£6.99
Ugenia Lavender and the Burning Pants	978-0-230-70143-4	£6.99
Ugenia Lavender: Home Alone	978-0-230-70144-1	£6.99
Ugenia Lavender and the Temple of Gloom	978-0-230-70145-8	£6.99
Ugenia Lavender: The One and Only	978-0-230-70146-5	£6.99

All Pan Macmillan titles can be ordered from our website, www.panmacmillan.com, or from your local bookshop and are also available by post from:

Bookpost, PO Box 29, Douglas, Isle of Man IM99 1BQ
Credit cards accepted. For details:
Telephone: 01624 677237
Fax: 01624 670923
Email: bookshop@enterprise.net
www.bookpost.co.uk

Free postage and packing in the United Kingdom